# SAM AND VIOLET ARE TWINS

### By
## Nicole Rubel

A Snuggle & Read Story Book

AN AVON  CAMELOT BOOK

# To my twin sister, Bonnie

SAM AND VIOLET ARE TWINS is an original publication of Avon Books. This work has never before appeared in book form.

AVON BOOKS
A division of
The Hearst Corporation
959 Eighth Avenue
New York, New York 10019

First Camelot Printing, April, 1981

CAMELOT TRADEMARK REG. U.S. PAT. OFF. AND IN
OTHER COUNTRIES, MARCA REGISTRADA, HECHO EN U.S.A.

Printed in the U.S.A.

BAN  10 9 8 7 6 5 4 3

SAM

VIOLET

Sam and Violet are twins.

They have the same blue eyes and
the same brown fur.

The same size noses and the same soft paws.

But they are not the same at all.

One day, Sam and Violet walked into
their classroom late.

"Oh, here are the twins!" said their
teacher, Mr. Moose.

"Since Violet is behind in her addition, I'm giving you both extra homework."

"Mr. Moose," said Sam, "*I'm* not behind in my arithmetic."

"But you and Violet are twins and you can go home and work on it together," said Mr. Moose.

"Ugh," said Sam.

As they walked home from school, Sam said, "I've been thinking, Violet."

"We wear the same clothes, we have the same friends, and everyone thinks we're alike."

"I wonder who I am," said Sam.

"I wonder who I am too," said Violet.

At home their mother greeted them.
"Hello, twins. Guess who's here? Your
Aunt Rose and Uncle Ross."

"Look," said Aunt Rose. "Aren't the twins the cutest kittens in their matching clothes?"

"Stand back to back!" said Uncle
Ross. "I want to see which twin is taller."

"Please call me Violet!" said Violet.

"Please call me Sam!" said Sam.

"Hmm," said Uncle Ross. "I wonder what's bothering the twins!"

Later during dinner, Mom said, "I
don't think the twins were nice to their
Aunt Rose and Uncle Ross today."

"Don't you like your aunt and uncle?"
asked Dad.

"Oh," sighed Violet. "I love Aunt Rose and Uncle Ross."

"Sam and I are unhappy because we want to be called Sam and Violet and not the twins."

"I'm sure we can solve this problem,"
said Mom.

The next Saturday Mom and Dad
took Sam and Violet shopping.

They picked out their own outfits for
the first time.

Sam looked around the store and

tried on a sailor suit.

Violet searched and found a yellow

sweat shirt with polka dots.

On the way home Dad made a
promise.

"Sam," he said, "Tomorrow you and I
will go fishing."

And Mom said, "Violet, let's plant our own vegetable garden."

"I feel much better now," said Sam.

"Me too," said Violet. "And I'm glad we're twins."